Winnie the Witch

Text copyright © 1987 by Valerie Thomas

Illustrations copyright © 1987 by Korky Paul

A hardcover edition of this book was first published in
the United Kingdom by Oxford University Press in 1987.
Manufactured in Singapore. All rights reserved.
For information address HarperCollins Children's Books, a division of HarperCollins Publishers,
1350 Avenue of the Americas, New York, NY 10019.
www.harpercollinschildrens.com

Library of Congress Cataloging-in-Publication Data is available.
ISBN-10: 0-06-117312-6 (trade bdg.) — ISBN-13: 978-0-06-117312-7 (trade bdg.)

Typography by Rachel L. Schoenberg
1 2 3 4 5 6 7 8 9 10
❖
First HarperCollins Edition, 2007

WINNIE THE WITCH

By Valerie Thomas

Illustrated by Korky Paul

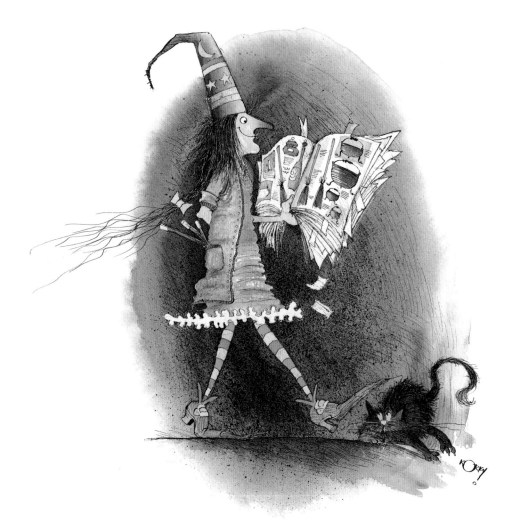

HarperCollins Publishers

Winnie the Witch lived in
a black house in the forest.
The house was black on the
outside and black on the inside.
The carpets were black.
The chairs were black.
The bed was black, and it had
black sheets and black blankets.
Even the bathtub was black.

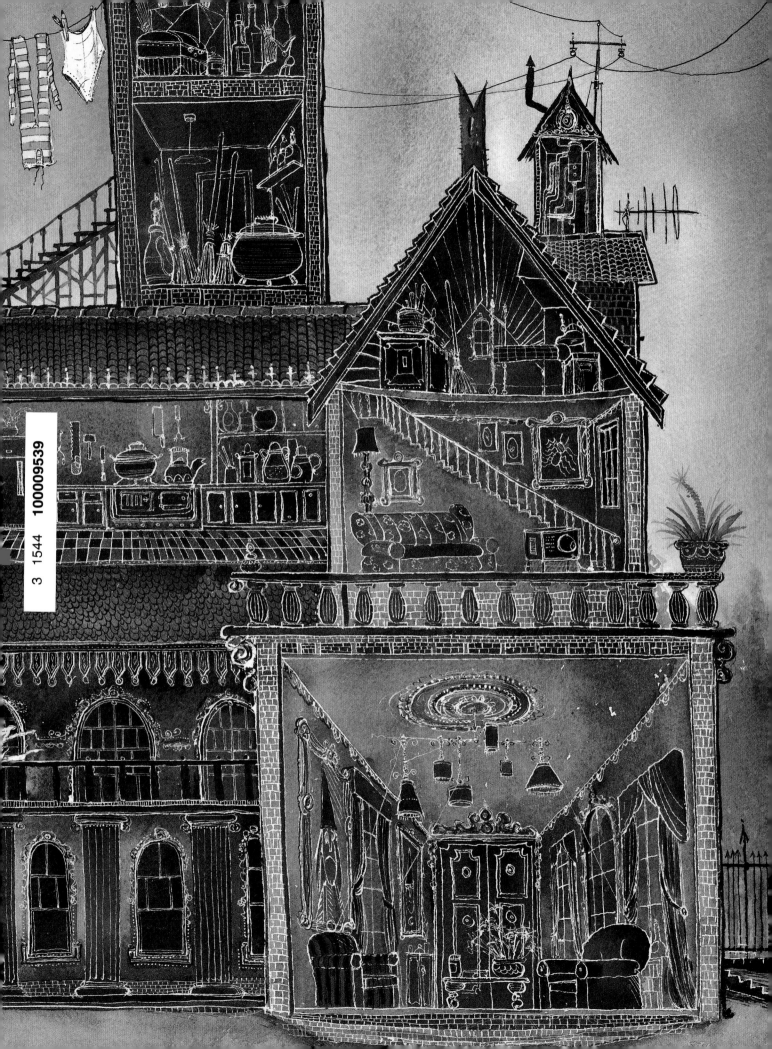

Winnie lived in her black
house with her cat, Wilbur.
He was black too. And that
is how the trouble began.

When Wilbur sat on the carpet with
his eyes open, Winnie could see him.
She could see his eyes, anyway.

But when Wilbur closed
his eyes and went to sleep,
Winnie couldn't see him at all.
So she tripped over him.

One day, after a nasty fall,
Winnie decided something
had to be done. She picked
up her magic wand, waved it
once, and ABRACADABRA!
Wilbur was a black cat no longer.
He was bright green!

ABRACADABRA!

Now, when Wilbur slept on
a chair, Winnie could see him.

When Wilbur slept on the
floor, Winnie could see him.

And she could see him
when he slept on the bed.
But Wilbur was not allowed
to sleep on the bed . . .

. . . so Winnie put
him outside.
Outside in
the grass.

Winnie came hurrying
outside, tripped over Wilbur,
turned three somersaults,
and fell into a rosebush.

When Wilbur sat outside
in the grass, Winnie couldn't
see him, even when his eyes
were wide open.

This time, Winnie was furious.
She picked up her magic wand,
waved it five times,
and . . .

... ABRACADABRA!
Wilbur had a red head,
a yellow body, a pink tail,
blue whiskers, and four purple legs.
But his eyes were still green.

Now Winnie could see Wilbur
when he sat on a chair,
when he lay on the carpet,
when he crawled into the grass ...

. . . and even when he
climbed to the top of
the tallest tree.

Wilbur climbed to the top
of the tallest tree to hide.
He looked ridiculous and he knew it.
Even the birds laughed at him.

Wilbur was miserable.
He stayed at the top
of the tree all day
and all night.

Next morning, Wilbur
was still up the tree.
Winnie was worried.
She loved Wilbur and
hated for him to be
miserable.

Then Winnie had an idea.
She waved her magic wand
and ABRACADABRA!
Wilbur was a black cat once more.
He came down from the tree,
purring.

Then Winnie waved her wand
again, and again, and again.

ABRACADABRA!

Now, instead of a black house,
she had a yellow house with a
red roof and a red door.
The chairs were white with
red-and-white cushions.
The carpet was green with
pink roses.

The bed was blue,
with pink-and-white
sheets and pink blankets.
The bathtub was a
gleaming white.

And now Winnie can
see Wilbur no matter
where he sits.